Introduction

The big book of *Yeah! Chinese!* contains various resources, which provides teaching recommendations, strategies, etc. to teach each story and new words.

For teacher's convenience, the big book provides contents as following:

Story's brief introduction helps teachers be familiar with the background of each story beforehand. And teachers can differentiate teaching by expanding more information in details from students' prior knowledge.

Main characters help teachers introduce the main characters to students beforehand and guide students into the story.

Learning objectives are prepared for teachers to set up clear daily goals for students.

New words teaching guides provide teachers with suggestions on the process, strategies and activities of introducing the new words.

Warming up provides suggestions on guiding the students to predict and follow the development of the story.

Story teaching guides provide suggestions and hints to help teachers ask key points of the materials.

Hints such as teaching skills, review activities, classroom management methods, culture elements and the fun points of the stories will help teachers to prepare lessons.

Needed videos (with the logo ▶) during teaching can be found on the official website.

How to use Yeah! Chinese! to teach Chinese?

General guidelines for the procedure of a story lesson

If it is a 3 teaching periods per week, it is suggested to teach with following steps: **First period,** teach new words with song and do the activity about the targeted vocabulary. **Second period,** review the new words, song and predict the cover page of the story; and start the new story. **The last period,** do activities about the targeted vocabulary, and retell the story or do a role play.Teachers may do any changes according to class progress.

Ways to teach new words

- Teach action words such as run, catch, take, etc. with body gestures or movements. For example, when introducing the new word "run", the teacher runs at same time.
- Show the flashcards of the new words to establish meaning as an additional visual aid.
- Teach new words with most familiar songs or melodies. For example, when teaching "stand up and sit down", the teacher can sing "stand up and sit down" repeatedly with the "Ten little Indians" melody.
- Use fun activities to help students memorize new words in a low anxiety atmosphere. For example, when teaching the word "bite", ask students to walk around a circle or walk like an animal in the classroom by saying "bite".

Ways to teach story

- Prepare question word cards with Pinyin and English meaning when asking questions. When asking a question, point to the question word to establish the meaning every time.
- Introduce the main characters. e.g. He is Tom. She is Nini. Then ask students what the main characters' names are.
- Start the story from the cover. When asking questions to students, point to the question word to provide clear meaning every time. e.g. What does she say? Who is singing? Is he singing or is she dancing?
- In the middle of the story use 5-wh question words to develop or to bed the story.
- Let students predict the ending. e.g. Who feels hurt? The brother or the sister?
- Sometimes create a pause or wait time to let students finish the sentence or for a tense moment.
- Use sounds and visual tools. Capture students' attention with surprise sound effects. For example, when the students need to say "wow", teach them to use funny sound effect for "wow".
- Maintain eye contact. It will draw students' attention when the teacher makes eye contact with them.
- Use multiple ways of movement. For example, when the students hear the new words such as "be quiet", they need to show "quiet" gesture. As the storyteller, the teacher can "paint" pictures with his / her hands, feet, legs and head.
- Change your voice with different characters. Voice is one of the best ways to bring the character to life and gets students' attention immediately.
- Use props. Don't introduce the props all at once, but bring them out one by one during poignant parts in the telling.

Ways to teach song

- Slow & body movements are the key methods to teach song.
- First of all, let students listen to the melody by demonstrating with body movement.
- The teacher demonstrates singing the song line by line slowly.
- Invite students as a song leader to guide others for singing.
- Sing fast or slow, higher or lower for fun. Let students sing very slowly or sing faster each time to exaggerate the tempo.
- Humming the song. When students are familiar with the song, let them hum the song, which make the song more attractive for them to sing.
- Magic claps or stamp feet. When hearing assigned words, students need to clap hands or "be quiet" or stamp feet. After couple time of practices, then have a competition.
- Play games when singing a song.

Ways to teach games

- Games are played in very class period as a review for the language.
- Model the game before it starts. Invite one or two students to demonstrate how to play the game.
- Explain teacher's expectations before the games.
- Prepare the props or flashcards beforehand for the games.

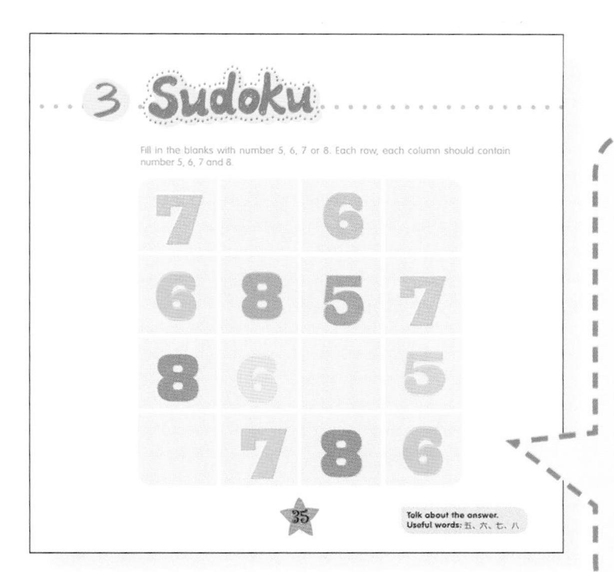

How to use activities

- Activities are designed to reinforce students' speaking and listening skills.
- Model before starting the activity.
- Prepare the activities with diversified requirements to achieve the maximum benefit of the activity.
- Provide students with more practice in the process by having them share the answers with their partners before answering the class.

Ways to retell a story / do a role play

- Pair up students to retell the story with the retelling page.
- Pair up students. When a student describes the picture randomly, another one points to the picture accordingly.
- Invite students to act out the story either with props or character cards.
- Let students use props or a stage theater to retell the story or do a role play which help some students who are shy to present in low anxiety.

Word list

	New words	English	Lesson
B	八(分)	eight (points)	3
D	得	get	3
J	九(下)	nine (times)	4
L	六	six	2
M	沒有	none	2
P	拍	dribble	4
Q	七(分)	seven (points)	3
S	十(下)	ten (times)	4
X	小熊	little bear	4
Z	找到 捉迷藏	found hide and seek	1 1

How to use word list

Students themselves can use the word list to review and monitor what they have learned after class. The teacher can use it to check if the students have mastered the words or not. A better way of checking is to combine the word list with flashcards. For example, students should find the correct flashcard when the teacher says a word at random.

Contents

1 捉迷藏 Hide and seek 5

2 我拿六个玩具
I take six toys 13

3 我得七分 I get seven points 21

4 拍球 Dribble the ball 29

Word list

Lesson 1
捉迷藏
Hide and Seek

故事简介

小朋友们在公园里玩儿。Helen 建议玩儿捉迷藏。“五、四、三、二、一”，Helen 找到了 Aiko 和 Jenny，但是 Nini 在哪里呢?

教学目标

1. 掌握词语“捉迷藏”。
2. 掌握词语“找到”。

主要人物

生词教学

• 捉迷藏

1. 领读。
2. 观看视频 ，让学生说一说视频中的动物、人物在玩儿什么。
3. 借助课本 P9 的歌曲练习词语。

小提示

在确认安全的前提下，教师可带学生到学校游乐场玩儿捉迷藏。

• 找到

1. 领读。（动作演示。）
2. 借助课本 P12 的活动练习词语。

小提示

1. 可以配合动词“捉迷藏”做活动。
2. 准备一些实物（帽子、蛋糕、苹果、彩色笔）藏在教室里，让学生找一找，找到的学生要大声说“找到……了”。

New words

- 捉迷藏
  hide and seek
- 找到
  found

学过的词：
我们……吧、玩儿、一、二、三、四、五、在、哪里

故事热身

提问

1. 谁推 Aiko？（指着 Aiko 的妈妈问。）
2. Jenny 和 Nini 可能说什么？（指着 Jenny 和 Nini 问。）
3. Nini 在做什么？（指着 Nini 问。）
4. 小狗在哪里？（指着小狗问。）

小提示

1. 借助书中的人物图介绍故事主要人物：Aiko、Jenny、Nini 和 Helen。
2. 教师准备英文图卡解释可能用到的、学生没学过的词语。

提问

1. 这里有几个人？（让学生数一数。）
2. 你喜欢玩儿捉迷藏吗？（让学生说一说。）

提问

1. Helen 说什么？（指着 Helen 问。）
2. Helen 为什么要用手挡着眼睛？（指着 Helen 做动作提问。）

小提示

提示学生注意 Aiko、Jenny、Nini 和 Helen 跑开的方向，让学生猜一猜她们会藏到哪里。

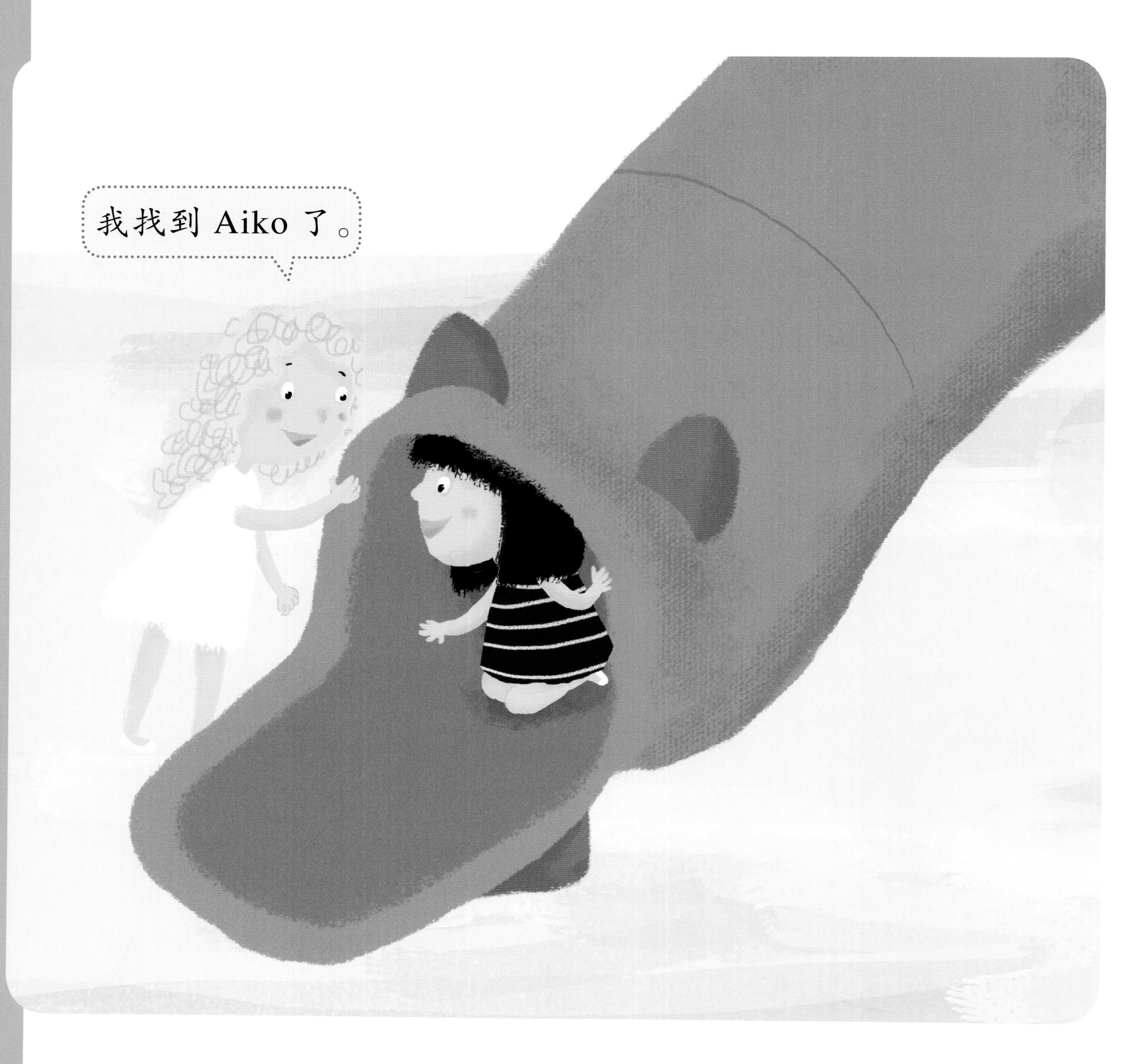

提问

1. Helen 找到几个人了？（指着 Helen 问。）
2. Aiko 喜欢玩儿捉迷藏吗？（让学生说一说。）

提问

1. Helen 找到几个人了？（指着 Helen 问。）
2. Nini 在哪里？（让学生说一说。）

提问

1. Aiko、Helen 和 Jenny 说什么？（指着 Aiko、Helen 和 Jenny 问。）
2. 谁找到 Nini 了？（让学生说一说。）

小提示

提示学生注意 Nini 和小狗的表情和动作，让学生猜一猜她想对小狗说什么。

Lesson 2

我拿六个玩具

I take six toys

故事简介

小朋友们在教室里玩儿玩具。桌子上摆着各种各样的玩具。Bobo、Alan 和 Tom 把玩具拿光了，John 没有玩具，急得直跺脚。Bobo 把他的变形金刚分给了 John。

教学目标

1. 掌握数字“六”。
2. 掌握常用词语“没有”。

主要人物

John

Bobo

Alan

Tom

生词教学

- 六

1. 展示图片或手势示意。
2. 观看视频 ▶ ，一起数一数。
3. 让学生写一写“六”。

小提示

1. 可带领学生复习“一、二、三、四、五”。
2. 借助课本 P23 的活动做练习。

- 没有

1. 领读。（动作演示。）
2. 借助课本 P24 的活动做练习。

小提示

“猜一猜”小游戏：让学生两人一组，每組分一张小纸片，其中一个学生把纸片藏在手里，把手藏在背后，然后伸出手让另一个同学猜纸片在哪只手里，如果没猜中要大声说“没有”。

New words

- 六
  six
- 没有
  none

学过的词：我、拿、玩具、两个、四个

故事热身

提问

1. 教室里有几个小朋友？（让学生数一数。）
2. 桌子上有什么玩具？你想拿什么玩具？（让学生说一说。）

小提示

1. 借助书中的人物图介绍故事主要人物：John、Bobo、Alan和Tom。
2. 教师准备英文图卡解释可能用到的、学生没学过的词语。
3. 复习“拿”“玩具”和学过的数字。老师准备一些小玩具，从玩具中抓出几个，让学生猜一猜老师拿走了几个玩具。

Story

提问

1. Bobo 拿几个玩具？（指着 Bobo 问。）
2. Bobo 拿什么玩具？（指着 Bobo 问。）

小提示

提示学生注意 Bobo 拿两个玩具后还剩几个玩具，让学生说一说。

提问

1. Alan 拿几个玩具？（指着 Alan 问。）
2. Alan 拿什么玩具？（指着 Alan 问。）

小提示

提示学生注意 Alan 拿四个玩具后还剩几个玩具，让学生说一说。

提问

1. Tom 拿几个玩具？（指着 Tom 问。）
2. Tom 拿什么玩具？（指着 Tom 问。）

提问

1. John 说什么？（指着 John 问。）
2. John 为什么跺脚？（指着 John 问。）

提问

1. John 说什么？（指着 John 问。）
2. Bobo 为什么给 John 玩具？（让学生说一说。）

小提示

提示学生注意 Bobo 的的表情，让学生猜一猜他会说什么。

Lesson 3
我得七分
I get seven points

故事简介

Aiko、Tom、Helen 和 Henry 分成两组玩儿扔球比赛。Aiko 和 Tom 一组，Helen 和 Henry 一组。Henry 原本以为要赢了，但其实他把球扔到了 Aiko 和 Tom 这一组的板子上。

教学目标

1. 掌握动词“得”。
2. 掌握数字“七（分）”“八（分）”。

主要人物

生词教学

- **得**

1. 领读。
2. 借助课本 P33 的歌曲练习词语。

- **七（分）**

1. 领读。（展示图片或手势示意。）
2. 观看视频，一起数一数。
3. 让学生写一写"七"。

小提示

教师可以自制一个九宫格纸板，在格子里写上"1、2、3、4、5、6、7、8、9"，然后将学生分组比赛扔球，哪一组扔中的数字相加之和最多，哪一组就赢了。

小提示

借助课本 P36 的活动练习词语。

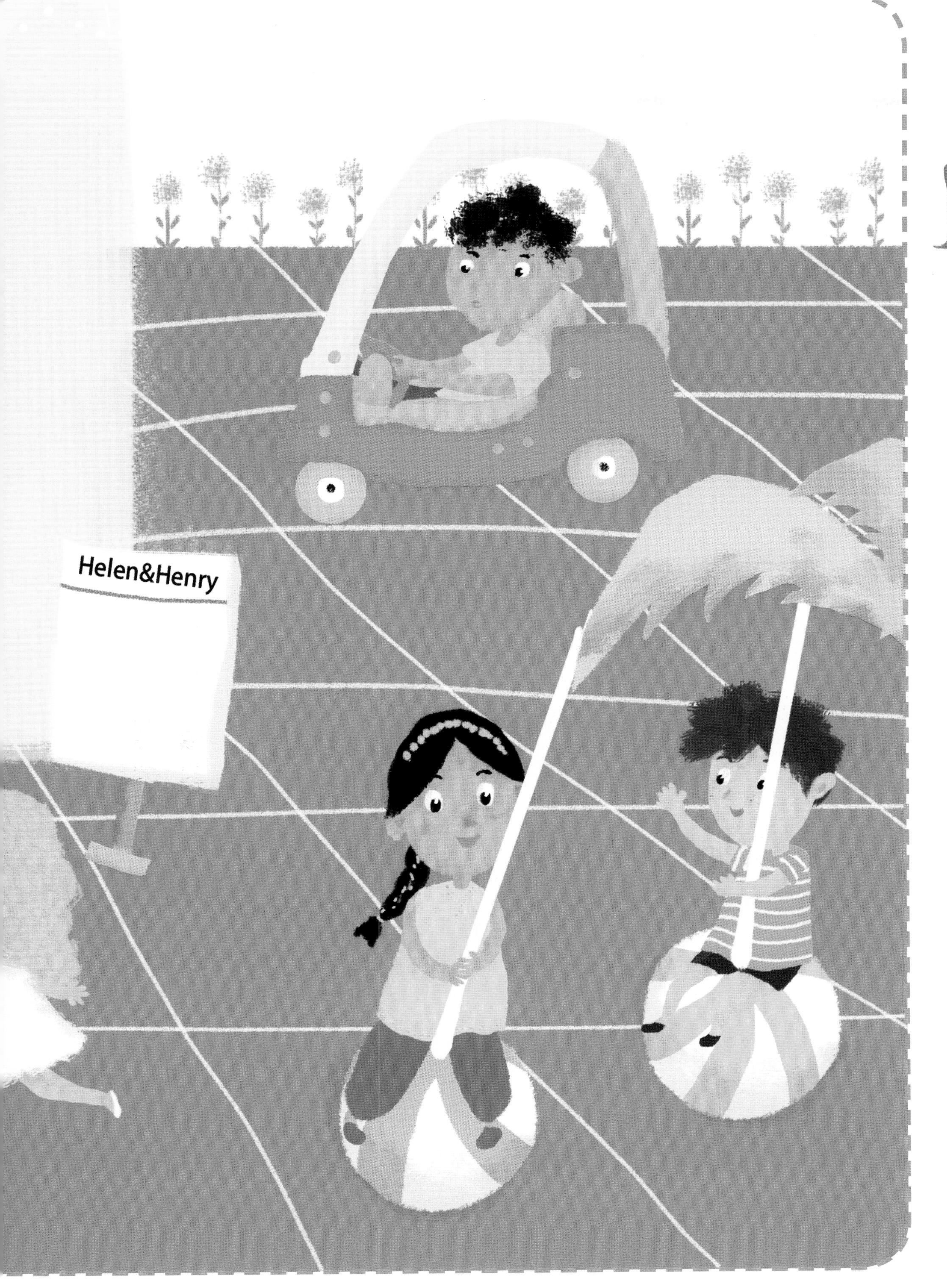

New words

- 得
  get
- 七（分）
  seven (points)
- 八（分）
  eight (points)

学过的词：我、我们、三、五、赢了

- 八（分）

1. 领读。（展示图片或手势示意。）
2. 观看视频，一起数一数。
3. 让学生写一写“八”。

小提示

借助课本 P34 的游戏练习词语。

故事热身

提问

1. 活动室里有几个小朋友？（让学生数一数。）
2. Bobo 在玩什么？（指着 Bobo 问。）
3. Aiko 和 Tom 一组，他们的球是什么颜色的？Henry 和 Helen 一组，他们的球是什么颜色的？（分别指着他们的球问。）

小提示

1. 借助书中的人物图介绍故事主要人物：Aiko、Tom、Henry 和 Helen。
2. 教师准备英文图卡解释可能用到的、学生没学过的词语。
3. 提示学生注意墙上纸板上的数字，让学生读一读。

提问

1. Aiko 得几分？（指着纸板问。）
2. Tom 为什么竖起大拇指？（指着 Tom 做动作问，让学生说一说。）

小提示

提示学生注意 Tom 的表情和手势，让学生说一说 Tom 想对 Aiko 说什么。

提问

1. Tom 得几分？（指着纸板问。）
2. Aiko 和 Tom 的组得几分？（指着纸板问。）
3. Aiko 厉害还是 Tom 厉害？（让学生说一说。）
4. Helen 和 Henry 为什么大笑？（指着 Helen 和 Henry 问。）

小提示

提示学生注意 Aiko、Tom、Helen 和 Henry 的表情，让学生说一说他们的表情一样不一样，为什么。

提问

1. Helen 得几分？（指着纸板问。）
2. Henry 写什么？（指着 Henry 问。）

小提示

提示学生注意 Helen 的表情和动作，让学生说一说她开心不开心。

提问

1. Henry 得几分？（指着纸板问。）
2. Henry 厉害吗？（让学生说一说。）

提问

1. 球在哪里？（指着纸板问。）
2. 谁得分？（让学生说一说。）
3. Helen 和 Henry 得几分？（指着记分板问。）
4. Aiko 说什么？（指着 Aiko 问。）

小提示

1. 提示学生注意两组的得分，让学生说一说为什么 Aiko 和 Tom 赢了。
2. 提示学生注意 Aiko 和 Helen 的表情和动作，让学生说一说她们的表情一样不一样，为什么。

Lesson 4
拍球
Dribble the ball

故事简介

大象、小牛、小马和小熊一起到郊外的草地上玩儿拍球游戏。小熊和小牛拍得很好，大象也鼓足劲想大展身手，但是轮到大象拍球时，它不小心用力太大，球飞走了。小牛、小熊和小马生气地看着飞走的球，大象感到很不好意思。

教学目标

1. 认识动物“小熊”。
2. 掌握常用词语“拍”。
3. 掌握数字“九（下）”“十（下）”。

主要人物

大象

小牛

小马

小熊

生词教学

- **小熊**

1. 领读。（展示图片。）
2. 观看视频 ▶，问一问学生喜不喜欢小熊。

小提示

1. 带领学生复习学过的动物名词。
2. 让学生画一画小熊。

- **拍**

1. 领读。（展示图片或动作演示。）
2. 观看视频 ▶，问一问学生视频中的小朋友们在做什么。
3. 借助课本 P45 的歌曲练习词语。

小提示

1. “老师说”小游戏：让学生听老师指令，当老师说“老师说‘拍头’”时，学生就拍头，当老师说“老师说‘拍手’时”，学生就拍手，以此类推。学生如果没有听到“老师说”三个字就不可以动。老师可以带领学生复习身体词语。注意提醒学生要轻轻地拍。
2. 借助课本 P48 的活动练习词语。

New words

- 小熊
  little bear
- 拍
  dribble
- 九（下）
  nine (times)
- 十（下）
  ten (times)

学过的词： 大象、小牛、球、飞走了

• 九（下）

1. 领读。（展示图片或手势示意。）
2. 观看视频，一起数一数。
3. 让学生写一写“九”。

• 十（下）

1. 领读。（展示图片或手势示意。）
2. 观看视频，一起数一数。
3. 让学生写一写“十”。

小提示

1. “拍球”小游戏：让学生一边拍球，一边数数字。拍了 9 下和 10 下的学生就自然到下一轮。没有拍到 9 下和 10 下的学生要帮忙数数。
2. “拍手”小游戏：老师可以先将学生分组，然后快速地拍手，让每组学生数老师拍了几下，并抢答，哪一组回答得又快又准，哪一组就赢了。
3. 借助课本 P46 的游戏练习词语。

故事热身

提问

1. 图中有什么动物？有几只小鸟？有几条鱼（指着动物问，让学生数一数。）
2. 它们要去做什么？（让学生说一说。）

小提示

1. 借助书中的人物图介绍故事主要人物：大象、小牛、小马和小熊。
2. 教师准备英文图卡解释可能用到的、学生没学过的词语。
3. 复习学过的动物名词和数字。

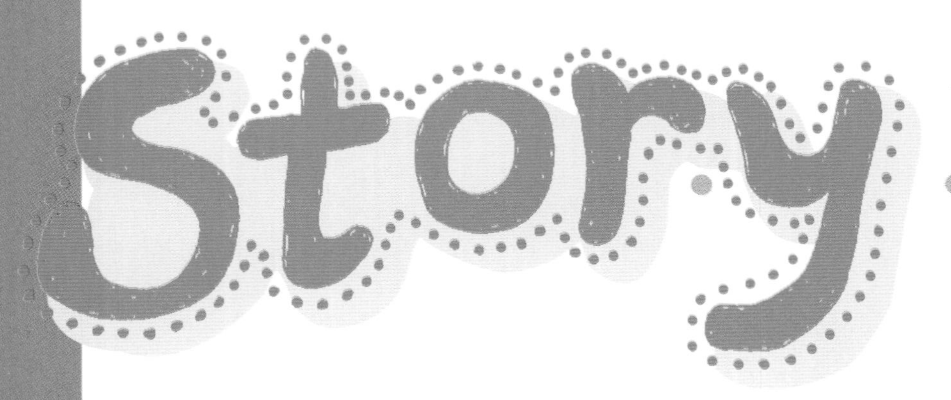

提问

1. 小熊在做什么？（指着小熊问。）
2. 小熊拍了几下？（指着小熊问。）
3. 图中有几只小鸟？（让学生数一数。）

小提示

提示学生注意小马、大象和小牛的表情和动作，让学生猜一猜它们可能对小熊说什么。

提问

1. 小牛在做什么？（指着小牛问。）
2. 小牛拍了几下？（指着小牛问。）
3. 小牛厉害还是小熊厉害？（让学生说一说。）

小提示

提示学生注意小鸟、小马、小熊和大象的表情和动作，让学生猜一猜大象厉害还是小牛厉害。

提问

大象拍了几下？（指着大象问。）

小提示

提示学生注意大象的表情和动作，让学生说一说大象用没用力拍球。

提问

小熊、小牛和小马为什么说“哎呀”？（让学生说一说。）

小提示

提示学生注意小熊、小牛和小马的表情和动作，让学生猜一猜发生了什么。

提问

1. 球怎么了？（指着球问。）
2. 大象会说什么？（让学生猜一猜。）

小提示

提示学生注意小牛、小熊和小马的表情和动作，让学生说一说它们怎么了。